To my grandmother Eleanora, whose chicks gave her
great comfort on the North Dakota prairie
P. M.

For Sue Anne
K. B.

❧

Text copyright © 2013 by Patricia MacLachlan
Illustrations copyright © 2013 by Kathryn Brown

First edition 2013

Library of Congress Cataloging-in-Publication Data is available.

Library of Congress Catalog Card Number pending

ISBN 978-0-7636-4753-7

12 13 14 15 16 17 SCP 10 9 8 7 6 5 4 3 2 1

Printed in Humen, Dongguan, China

This book was typeset in Adobe Jenson Pro.
The illustrations were done in watercolor.

Candlewick Press
99 Dover Street
Somerville, Massachusetts 02144

visit us at www.candlewick.com

Nora's Chicks

Patricia MacLachlan

illustrated by Kathryn Brown

Candlewick Press

When Nora came to America from Russia, she came with her mother, her father, and her baby brother, Milo. She brought a bag of clothes, two dolls, and her blanket. Her mother brought pictures of the country and family she had left behind, her favorite teacup, and three colorful tablecloths.

The prairie farm was not beautiful to Nora. There were no trees like the Russian trees, only one cottonwood by the river. There were no hills like the Russian hills.

Nora cried.

"Don't cry, Nora," said her father. "We'll plant trees."

"You can't plant a hill!" said Nora, crying harder.

The house was small, with old wooden floors that were worn smooth by the people who had lived there before. Nora's mother scrubbed the floors golden clean so Milo could crawl there. She took out all her pictures of Russia and hung them on the walls so Nora was surrounded by the trees and hills of the place she missed. Nora's mother took out the tablecloths and cut curtains for the windows, yellow and red and green. The house was full of color.

But still Nora was unhappy.

"There are not many people here," she told her mother. "There's no one to talk to."

"I will talk to you," said her mother, putting her arm around Nora. "And Milo will talk to you when he can talk."

Nora smiled for the first time.

"Yes, Milo will talk soon. But I need a friend now."

There was a house Nora could see from her upstairs window. It was far, but near enough to call whoever lived there a neighbor. One day a woman came from that house to visit. She brought a pie for Nora's family. And she brought her daughter, Susannah.

Nora and Susannah sat on the porch with their mothers. They walked to the barn to see the cows. But they didn't talk very much. Nora was shy. Susannah was shy, too.

Nora and her father drove their wagon to town to shop for flour and sugar and dried fruits for pie. The townspeople were nice. But they weren't Nora's friends. Nora and Susannah waved to each other when Nora's wagon passed Susannah's house. But they weren't friends, either.

One day a small dog came to the farm. He was thin and hungry. Nora went outside with Milo. She gave the dog a bowl of borscht. The dog ate it all and waited for more.

"He's our dog, Milo," said Nora. "We'll name him Willie, after Uncle Willie in Russia. Maybe he'll be my friend. I wish he could talk."

But Willie liked Milo best. When Milo walked, Willie followed him wherever he went. Willie came running when Milo fell down. He slept with Milo at night. "Willie" was Milo's first word. Willie was Milo's dog.

Nora's father bought more cows and another horse.
He plowed the fields with the horses. He milked the cows.
They were Father's cows and horses. Sometimes he sang
Russian lullabies to the cows when he milked them.
That made Nora sad.

"I need something all my own," Nora said to her mother
and father.

One day Father brought home some chicks and two geese
for eating.

"They are too beautiful to eat," said Nora.

"No, they are not," said her father.

"Yes," said Nora stubbornly. "Much too beautiful to eat."

Her father sighed. "All right, Nora. They are yours,"
he said. "Something all your own."

Nora called them all — even the geese — her chicks. They followed her when she walked. They watched everything she did. Sometimes they slept on the porch. Nora sang lullabies to them in Russian.

Her father looked at them hungrily. But he knew better. He couldn't eat them. They were Nora's chicks. And Nora had named them, every last one.

Natasha

Wolfgang

Irena

Eva

Polina

Susannah

Friend

Galina

Fritz

Clacker

Hoots

Ivan

Susannah was named after Susannah down the road.
Nora named one Friend because she wanted one.
Clacker and Hoots were the geese.

❧

Willie didn't eat them. He knew better, too. Sometimes he played with them or chased them. Once Willie fell asleep in the summer sunlight, chicks all around him, one nesting between his paws.

But still Nora was lonely. She took long walks, her chicks following.

"Look," people said when they drove by Nora in their wagons. "There's Nora and her chicks. Hello, Nora! Hello!"

Sometimes the chicks followed the horse and wagon. They had to be gathered up to ride with Nora.

And one Sunday, when Nora's family went to church, Nora and her father and mother and Milo walked up the aisle followed by a flock of chicks. Everyone laughed.

"Welcome," said the minister. "And welcome to Nora's chicks."

Later that day, Nora counted her chicks.

"Oh, no," cried Nora. "A chick is missing! Who is it? Where is it?" She looked behind the barn and under the shed and in the garden. She looked up the road and on the porch and all the way to the river.

All of a sudden, there was Susannah and Susannah's mother in their wagon.

"I brought you a lost chicken," called Susannah.

"Natasha!" exclaimed Nora. "I've looked everywhere for her!"

Natasha went squawking over to the rest of the chicks.

"You can bring her over to visit me anytime," said Susannah.

Nora looked at Susannah.

"Would you like to stay and play?" she asked.

"Yes," said Susannah. "I like your chicks, Nora. I wish I had chicks of my own."

Nora smiled and smiled. She didn't feel shy anymore.

"When my chicks have chicks of their own, I'll give you some," said Nora. "Then we'll both have chicks."

And while their mothers drank tea inside the house, surrounded by the pictures of Russian hills and trees, Susannah and Nora played outside with Milo and Willie.

Surrounded by blue sky.

Surrounded by prairie.

Surrounded by Nora's chicks.

DATE DUE

PRINTED IN U.S.A.